LA BEFANA

an Italian night after Christmas

An Italian tradition, adapted by
Sunday Frey-Blanchard
Illustrated by Roger Frey

Thanks to Treasure Frey and Roger Frey for all the hard work and advice. Thanks to Rhonda Gaudette, editor and madrina, for the spelling, grammar and sanity checks, freely offered and much needed. Thanks to Carolyn Frey, Master Storyteller and child whisperer. Thanks to the family for their patience and support and inspiration.

Visit www.booksurge.com to order additional copies.

ISBN: 9781419677427
Library of Congress Control Number: 2007937079

For my miracles, and wonderous epiphanies ~SFB

Off on the farthest edge,
of the smallest of towns,
Lived tiny Strega Befana in
the cleanest house all around.

She kept to herself away from the bustle,
sweeping her house through the mid-winter
hustle.

Villagers would come for toys, potions...

or baked sweets.....

She would mix and bake for them, then send them away with their treats.

Befana disliked visitors and never asked them to stay. She led a clean, quiet life and preferred it that way.

With a faded black scarf, she drew back her hair; and in plain skirt and strong boots, polished and swept every stair.

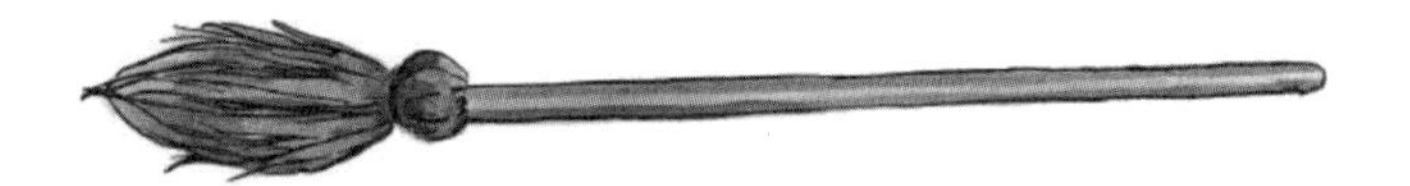

As she started to close up
one cold mid-winter night,
Befana pulled in the lantern
and blew out the light.

She was startled from her
work by a knock at the door.
"Visitors, now? No one had
come so late before."

She peeked out to see a
learned looking old man.
He was brilliantly dressed
and his face was quite tan.

Though his clothes were bright colors, they showed wear from the road. His shoes were all muddied and his weariness showed.

She opened the door, stepping cautiously aside. The man and his dirty shoes came swiftly inside.

“Good evening,” he said, “I do apologize that its late but I am in a hurry and lost and my mission is great.”

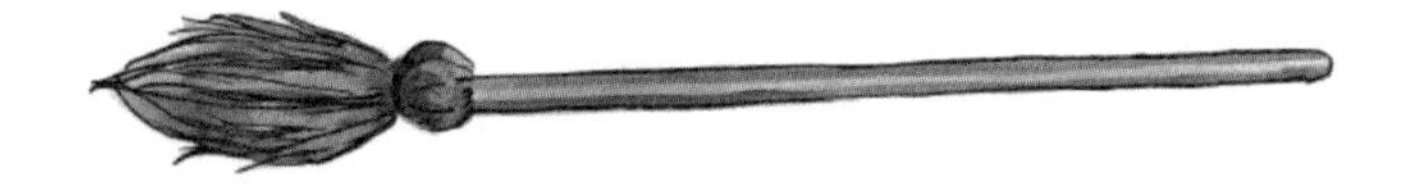

"I have seen a sign that a child has been born, one that will lead us all through a dark storm.

This child is divine, full of joy, hope and love. He is radiant and kind and sent from above.

I come bearing gifts to honor this child and to pledge my heart to this king who is mild.

You could come with us, these things that you sell as gifts for a king, would be suited quite well."

Befana was concerned about this man, and these signs, and didn't like the way firelight danced in his eyes.

Perhaps he was crazy, she thought with a sigh, after all, he was traveling beneath a wild, starry sky.

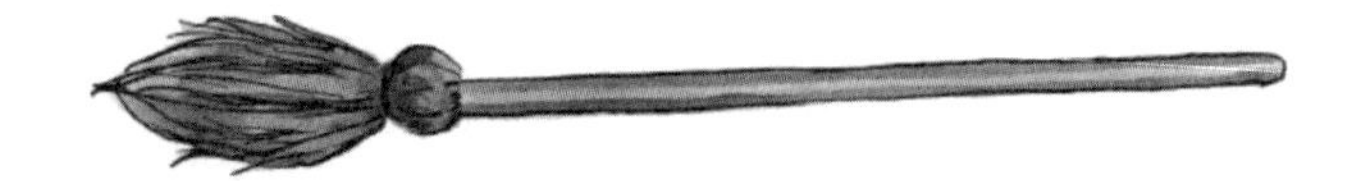

She could not help, she said
firmly and ushered him out,
she knew nothing of the child he
was speaking about.

Once he was gone, she slammed
the door shut, and reached for her
broom to sweep out the soot.

She started to sweep his dirt from her floor, when once again came a knock on the heavy oak door.

Another man, she saw through the door,
but this time with the finely dressed man, came many more.

“What do you want?” she asked, through the door’s heavy wood. “I need directions, my lady, and supplies if you could.”

The gentleman and his companions stomped roughly inside. Their boots were caked heavily with grime from the ride.

“My lady we are seeking a child of light. He will be a king for whom we can all fight.

We go to bring gifts and offer our hands, you are welcome to join us, as we cross through these lands.”

Once more she assured them she could be of no help. They paid for supplies, and she saw them all out.

Befana looked at the mess and slowly set down her broom. She'd take a quick nap before she tidied the room.

But her nap was sadly not to be long,
For once more the oak door was pounded upon.

“Go away!” she cried, without opening the door, “I know nothing about this child you search for.”

“Please leave at once. I will not come along, And no toys or bread will be given away for a song.”

Whoever had knocked, went slowly away, and Befana finally finished cleaning up for the day.

Muttering and sighing she swept the dirt out, but as she turned ‘round, she let out a small shout.

Out in the distance, something bright caught her eye, a wonderous new star, sparkled in the deep blue sky.

The star warmed her heart and she knew right away, it was no ordinary star and this no ordinary day.

Her thoughts raced back to those gentlemen, lost; their new born king and the lands they had crossed.

Something happened that moment, no one could have guessed, certainly not those men so gaily dressed.

She had an epiphany, and deep in her heart, she knew it wasn't yet, to late to start.

She laid out her plan, for this child king of light would have one more visitor if the signs turned out right.

Swiftly she gathered all the treasures she'd need. Gifts for the child would be her good deed.

She stowed away all the gifts in her bag, sweet breads and bright trinkets, until the bag sagged.

She was off through the door, she knew not to linger, her lantern and broomstick now grasped in her fingers.

Her eyes scanned the road and returned to the skies. The brightly lit beacon, once more filled her eyes.

She ran light and fast, with no sign of the men, or the child that they searched for, the one who would be king.

Her gifts, in a bundle, were clasped to her chest as fearfully lost, she stopped for a rest.

There was no sign to follow as she looked all around, in the stillness of night, she heard not a sound.

The guiding star in the velvety night
she could no longer see,
for millions of stars now shown
above the trees.

As she turned to go on, through a window she spied, a small sleeping child with closed, dreaming eyes.

Could this be the child? Her heart made a leap. Then she saw others beside him, also fast asleep.

Looking closer, she saw more babes in their beds. All over town there'd be children, winter dreams in their heads.

How could she know that she had found the right boy? Smiling, she chose to give each a new toy.

And so, she left, at the foot of each bed,
some of her trinkets and a piece of sweet bread.

She left something there for each good girl and boy, hoping one of them would be the child of light and pure joy.

She paused for a moment, and looked at the room, then, quick movements she made, sweeping up with her broom.

As she ran off to the next house, strong winds lifted her, til soon...

She was flying near the stars, and perched on her broom.

As she flew on her quest for the child of the light, her heart grew in her chest, and made her eyes glisten bright.

She gazed down upon the small sleeping children, and smiled, as a thought, to her mind came, unbidden.

Her child king of light was not truly hidden, for a small bit resided in each of these children.

So she kissed them all sweetly and tucked them in tight. There were many more children to see to that night.

Then she leapt to her broom to finish
her flight, knowing somehow she had still
found her child of the light.

Made in the USA
Middletown, DE
29 November 2024